My F

by Maryellen Gregoire

Nancy E. Harris, M.Ed—Reading
National Reading Consultant

capstone
classroom
Heinemann Raintree • Red Brick Learning
division of Capstone

I have a family.

I have a mother.

I have a father.

I have a sister.

I have a brother.

I have a grandmother.

I have a grandfather.

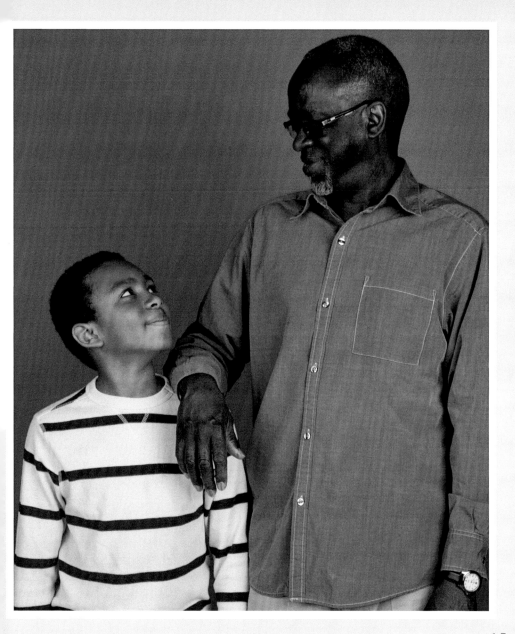

I have a dog.